KEKE MISSES HOME

Printed in the United Kingdom

ISBN: 9798544873020 (Paperback)

Printed in United Kingdom

First printing 2021. Published by Lenoir Publishing

www.lenoirfoundation.com

"You can find magic wherever you look. Sit back and relax, all you need is a book."

-Dr Seuss

Once upon a time,
there lived a little happy and exciting
young girl named Keke.

She loved going to school to be with her
friends and to learn new things. And when
she wasn't at school, Keke enjoyed
spending time with her parents.

She also liked riding her bike throughout her neighborhood and saying HELLO to all her neighbors.

Keke loved her life and there was nothing more she could ask for.

But one day, her mother and father came into her room after dinner and said, "Something new and exciting is happening for us!"

Keke's eyes widened and her face glowed. She couldn't wait to hear what would come out her parents' mouths next.

Maybe they were getting her a dog.
Or maybe they were finally going to
have her a baby brother or sister.

"We're moving to Uganda!"
Keke's dad said excitedly.

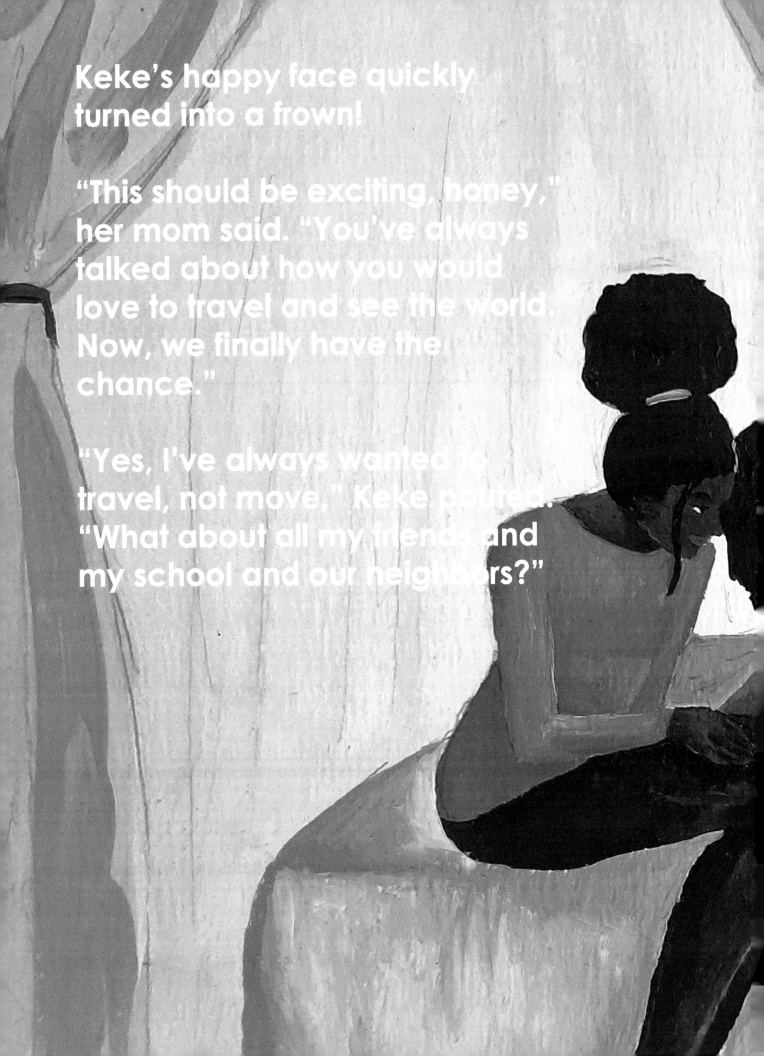

Keke's happy face quickly turned into a frown!

"This should be exciting, honey," her mom said. "You've always talked about how you would love to travel and see the world. Now, we finally have the chance."

"Yes, I've always wanted to travel, not move," Keke pouted. "What about all my friends and my school and our neighbors?"

"Well, we will meet new people and you will make new friends," her dad said. "And we will be able to learn more about the culture."

"But why are we moving anyways?" Keke asked.

"Well, our company has expanded into East Africa, so I will be leading the organization in Uganda," her dad explained.

Keke nodded her head sadly.

"It'll be better than you think," her mom added with a smile.

When they finally arrived in Uganda, Keke didn't feel so great. Everything looked different and nothing reminded her of home.

She tugged on her mother's shirt and leaned her head on her shoulder.

WELCOME TO ENTEBBE INTER

Their new home was in a tiny village. The houses looked different from any Keke had ever seen.

As Keke's parents explored their new home, Keke wandered off into their new backyard.

Suddenly, Keke noticed a lady next door sitting cross-legged in a meditation pose with her eyes closed.

She looks like she is at peace, Keke thought.

Later that day, Keke had finished unpacking her boxes and putting most of her belongings away. And then she began to help her mom finish unpacking the other items they had.

"I'm going to head to town and grab us some dinner for this evening," her father announced.

"Excellent, dear, because I am starving," her mom said with a laugh.

After a while, Keke's mom said,
"We should take a break."

"That's a good idea," Keke said.

Keke went back outside to the backyard to get some fresh air and think about her old home.

As she thought about her friends, neighbors, and school, tears began to fall from her eyes.

"Child," Keke heard suddenly. "Child."

Keke stopped to look around
and then she saw the neighbor from
earlier looking in her direction.

"Are those tears of happiness or sadness
I see, child?" the older lady asked.

"Sadness," Keke answered.

"Ah, I see," the lady said. Her English was very colorful with her Ugandan accent. "Since you are new here, I assume you are missing home?"

Keke nodded as the older-lady walked from her yard to get closer to Keke.

"Well, life is like that sometimes," the lady said. "My name is Miremba by the way."

"Nice to meet you, Miremba," Keke said sniffling.

"There, there, everything is going to be okay," Miremba said. "I think I know the perfect thing that will help you. Have you ever heard of mindfulness meditation?"

Keke shook her head.

"Well, it's when you train your mind to slow down all negative thoughts with breathing exercises or mantras," Miremba said with a big smile.

"What are mantras?" Keke asked as she began to dry her tears.

"A mantra is a chant that you can say to make yourself feel positive, gracious, motivated, or whatever you want to feel," Miremba answered.

"For example, one of my favorite mantras is 'Love the life you live'."

Keke looked slightly confused about everything the lady was telling her.

"Okay, let's try it together," Miremba said joyfully. "Close your eyes and take in a deep cleansing breath for 3 seconds and then exhale for 4 seconds."

Miremba inhaled and exhaled to show Keke what she meant. "This is the first thing we must do. And then we can repeat these breathing exercises a few more times, and then you can begin repeating the mantra in your head. Does that make sense?" Miremba asked.

"I think so," Keke said.

"Well, let's try it together," Miremba began. "Sometimes sitting helps." Miremba went to her house to grab two mats for her and Keke.

When she returned, she and Keke both sat on the mats and began breathing in and out.

"Now, let's begin saying the mantra out loud and then we can change to saying it in our heads," Miremba said.

"Love the life you live," they both began. "Love the life you live, love the life you live..."

They continued saying their mantra and eventually repeated it in their minds.

Suddenly, Miremba said, "As we bring this meditation to an end, let our minds be cleansed of negative thoughts. And so it is, Amen!"

Miremba and Keke opened their eyes. "How do you feel?" Miremba asked.

Keke couldn't quite describe the feeling, but she knew she felt much better than she had earlier that day.

"Happier," Keke answered with a smile.

"Excellent," Miremba said. "And the best part is that you can do this meditation anytime you feel the need."

Shortly, Keke's mom came outside and said, "Looks like you've already made a friend."

Keke's mom and Miremba introduced themselves to each other. And soon Keke's dad was back with their dinner.

"I got more than enough food, so how about you join us for dinner?" Keke's dad asked Miremba.

"I'd love to," Miremba said smilingly.

As Keke enjoyed dinner with Miremba and her parents, she thought to herself that maybe living in Uganda wouldn't be bad at all.

She thought of home, but this time, she was only wishing everyone well.

And after she was done, thinking about home, she thought about all the amazing things she would learn and people she would meet...

As this place would grow to become her new home.

The End

Proceeds from this book will be donated to the LeNoir Foundation.

LeNoir Foundation is a Non-profit organisation focused on rehabilitating public libraries in African countries. The mission is to give free and easy access to education for people. Our vision is that people should be able to access the knowledge everywhere. We have the goal to facilitate the access to books and other educational material to people in the need in Africa.

To know more about our initiative please visit: www.lenoirfoundation.com

Printed in Great Britain
by Amazon